kind

ginative

bitty ★ baby
shares
a gift

by Kirby Larson
& Sue Cornelison

★ American Girl®

Special thanks to Dr. Laurie Zelinger, consultant,
child psychologist, and registered play therapist.
Dr. Zelinger reviewed and helped shape the "For Parents"
section, which was written by editorial staff.

Questions or comments? Call 1-800-845-0005,
visit **americangirl.com,** or write to Customer Service,
American Girl, 8400 Fairway Place, Middleton, WI 53562-0497.

Printed in China
14 15 16 17 18 19 20 21 LEO 10 9 8 7 6 5 4 3 2 1

All American Girl and Bitty Baby marks are trademarks of American Girl.

Series Editorial Development: Erin Falligant and Jennifer Hirsch
Art Direction and Design: Gretchen Becker
Production: Jeannette Bailey, Judith Lary, William Mansfield, Paula Moon, Kristi Tabrizi

For Mom and Dad,
for everything
K.L.

To my stepdaughters,
Gina and Marcie, with love
S.C.

Bitty Baby and I finished wrapping Anna's birthday present.

"We're ready for the party!" I said.

At Anna's house, Bitty Baby and I put our present on the table. "She'll really like this one," I said.

Happy Birthday, Anna!

"A lot," said Bitty Baby. We ran to join the other girls.

First we played Pin the Wings on the Fairy.

Then we played Musical
Mushrooms and Fairy-Dust Relay.

After that we decorated cupcakes. Bitty Baby and
I used lots of fairy sprinkles. We ate ice cream and
drank fizzy Fairy Punch.

"Time for presents!" Anna said. She opened ours first. "I haven't read this yet. Thanks!"

I gave Bitty Baby a squeeze.
Anna *did* like our present!

Next was a puzzle. "I'm good at puzzles!" I said.

Anna opened another present.

"I have that game," I said, scooting closer. "Want me to show you how to play?"

"Not right now."

Anna unwrapped a stuffed giraffe.

"Oh, I love it!" She gave it a hug.

It was a very cute giraffe. "I could hold it
for you while you open the rest," I said.

"It's *my* birthday." Anna straightened her
fairy wings. "And these are *my* presents."

Anna's mother carried in a box with holes cut in the sides. "Here's one more!"

"It's just what I wanted!" Anna carefully lifted a kitten out of the box. "I'm naming her Princess."

Anna rolled a jingly ball. Princess batted at it with her little paws. Her tail wiggled as she played.

"Can I hold her?" Anna's sister asked.

"You're too little," Anna said.

"I'm the right size," I said. "And I'm very gentle."

Anna wrinkled her nose. "But it's my kitten. And I just got her."

Anna put Princess back into the box. "Let's play another game." She and the other girls ran off.

I stayed behind. "Anna's not being very nice," I said.

"She should share," said Bitty Baby.

We peeked into the box. Princess stretched out a paw. She really wanted to be picked up.

"A story might take our minds off Princess," I said.

"Good idea." Bitty Baby snuggled on my lap.

Once there was a fairy named Bitty Baby,
who was nice to everyone in the forest.
One day, she noticed Mouse hard at work.

"You're making a ladder!"
Bitty Baby exclaimed.

"So I can climb up to my new tree house."
Mouse put down her tiny hammer and
scampered up the twig ladder.

"That looks like a lot of
fun," said Bitty Baby.
"Can I play with you?"

Mouse wrinkled her nose. "Not right now."

Bitty Baby perched on a mossy stone.

Mouse scurried around. She admired the view from each window and door.

"Now can I come up?" asked Bitty Baby.

"It's *my* tree house," said Mouse. "But you could throw me that rope."

It was tied to a bucket of cheese and berries. Bitty Baby loved cheese and berries.

"How about now?" she asked.
"I threw you the rope."

Mouse didn't answer. Bitty Baby could hear her munching cheese and crunching berries.

She thought about sprinkling Mouse with fairy dust and turning her into a mushroom. That would show her!

But this was Mouse's tree house. She could choose when to share.

Bitty Baby settled in for a long wait.

Then Mouse leaned out a window. She looked very sad. "Something's wrong."

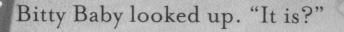

Bitty Baby looked up. "It is?"

"I have two chairs and a table and snacks. And I like being up high. But a tree house isn't as much fun as I thought it would be." Her whiskers drooped.

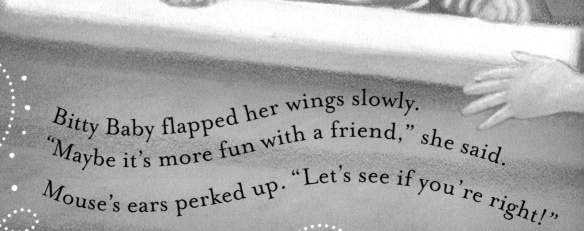

Bitty Baby flapped her wings slowly. "Maybe it's more fun with a friend," she said.

Mouse's ears perked up. "Let's see if you're right!"

Bitty Baby flew up to join her.

They ate cheese and berries and had such a lovely time that Mouse invited Bitty Baby to come back the very next week. She promised she would. The end.

"Mouse was nice," said Bitty Baby. "She shared."

"I bet Anna will, too," I said. "But this is her special day. She can choose when to share."

"Anyway, I've got a great idea!" Bitty Baby and I gathered up all the empty gift boxes and lots of tape.

"A castle for my Princess!" exclaimed Anna. "I love it."

Bitty Baby and I smiled.

Even Princess agreed it was *purrfect*.

For Parents

Sharing Basics

Just as your daughter is learning how to share, she's also realizing that sometimes it's OK *not* to share, such as when you're the birthday girl receiving special gifts. Help your daughter sort through the confusion by teaching her some rules and strategies for sharing.

About Borrowing

The next time you go to the library, ask the librarian to explain to your daughter the rules for borrowing. How long can she keep the books? What happens if she damages a book or returns it late?

Understanding the rules for borrowing helps your daughter learn that it's OK to set her own rules for sharing with friends. For instance, does she have toys in her room that shouldn't be played with outside? Do some of her electronic toys need to be turned off so that the batteries don't wear down?

Give your daughter opportunities to see *you* borrowing and sharing at home, too. Ask to "borrow" one of her markers to write a note, and offer to "share" your jewelry when she wants to play dress-up.

Planning for Playdates

Before your daughter has a playdate at home, remind her that her friend will want to play with the toys in her room. Ask if there are two or three special toys that she doesn't want to share. Allow her to tuck those toys away as long as she's willing to share the rest of her toys.

If your daughter does have trouble sharing during the playdate, ask "Can you two use your imaginations to think of a fair way to share that toy?" Consider setting a timer so that each has the same amount of time to play with the toy. Or put the toy away until they come up with a solution, and then praise them for being creative and finding a way to share fairly.

After the playdate, ask your daughter if she had fun sharing. What kinds of things did she and her friend play or do?

Before a Party

Before your daughter heads off to a birthday party, remind her that the birthday girl may not want to share her new things right away. Reread *Bitty Baby Shares a Gift,* and talk about how hard it is for the little girl to wait for Anna to share her toys. Then ask your daughter how she thinks Anna feels when the others want to play with her new things.

What might Anna be worried about? Is she afraid the other girls will lose the pieces to her new puzzle before she's able to put it together? Or that if they play with Princess, the kitten might get scared or hurt? Ask your daughter if she might feel that way, too, if she had a new pet to take care of.

For more parent tips, visit **americangirl.com/BittyParents**

Where the story ends, her imagination begins

Discover dolls to hug, books to share, and play sets to make the stories leap to life.

CI300188

Request your FREE catalogue!

Just mail this card, call 800-845-0005, or visit americangirl.com/catalogue.

Parent's name _____ Girl's birth date ___/___/___

Address _____

City _____ State _____ Zip _____

Parent's e-mail *By providing your e-mail address, you will receive e-mail updates and special offers from American Girl.*

(___) _____
Phone ❏ Home ❏ Work

Parent's signature _____ 12583i

Send a catalogue to a grandparent or friend:

Grandparent/adult's name _____

Address _____

City _____ State _____ Zip _____

Today's date ___/___/___ 12591i

play@
☆ American Girl™

Discover the online place with
games, quizzes, activities, and
more at americangirl.com/play.

☆ American Girl®

PO BOX 620497
MIDDLETON WI 53562-0497

curious

loving

confident